YOU WILL BE

MY FRIEND!

Peter Brown

Little, Brown and Company
New York Boston

Lucy was very excited when she woke up.

MOM!
I've decided I'm going to make a new friend today!
Isn't that exciting?

That IS exciting, Lucille. But how do you plan on finding a new friend?

Mom, the forest is crawling with fun critters. Surely ONE of them will want to be my friend.

This is going to be GREAT!

So Lucy went outside to begin her search.
Good luck, Lucille!
Bye, Mom!

I CANNOT WAIT
to make a new friend!

We're going to
do cartwheels!

And climb trees!

And have picnics!

And go swimming!

And have a
dance party!

Lucy's search got off to a great start when a nice critter invited her to play.

But things didn't work out.

Oh well, there are plenty of
other critters in the forest.

It didn't take long for Lucy to find another friendly-looking animal.

That friendship didn't work out either.

Lucy did her best to win over the forest animals.

She was helpful.

She asked lots of questions.

And she tried to fit in with everyone she met.

But Lucy was starting to feel ridiculous.

She came close to making friends a few times.

Thanks for inviting me to lunch!

But something always went wrong.

Lucy couldn't believe how hard it was to make a new friend. She was ready to be friends with ANYONE.

Well, almost anyone.

SQUEAK!
SQUEAK?

That's when things got ugly.

You WILL be my friend!

Lucy tried to calm
herself down.

Take a deep breath, Lucy!

You can do this.
You can make a new friend.

Just be yourself.

DOESN'T
WANT TO BE

ANYBODY

MY FRIEND?!

This is hopeless.

It looked as if Lucy would never find a new friend.

Squawk?
And then a funny thing happened.

Squawk?
Squawkity-Squawk?

OH! MY! GOSH! Are you asking me to be YOUR friend?!
SQUAWK!
I ACCEPT!

And that's the story of how these two friends found each other.

The End

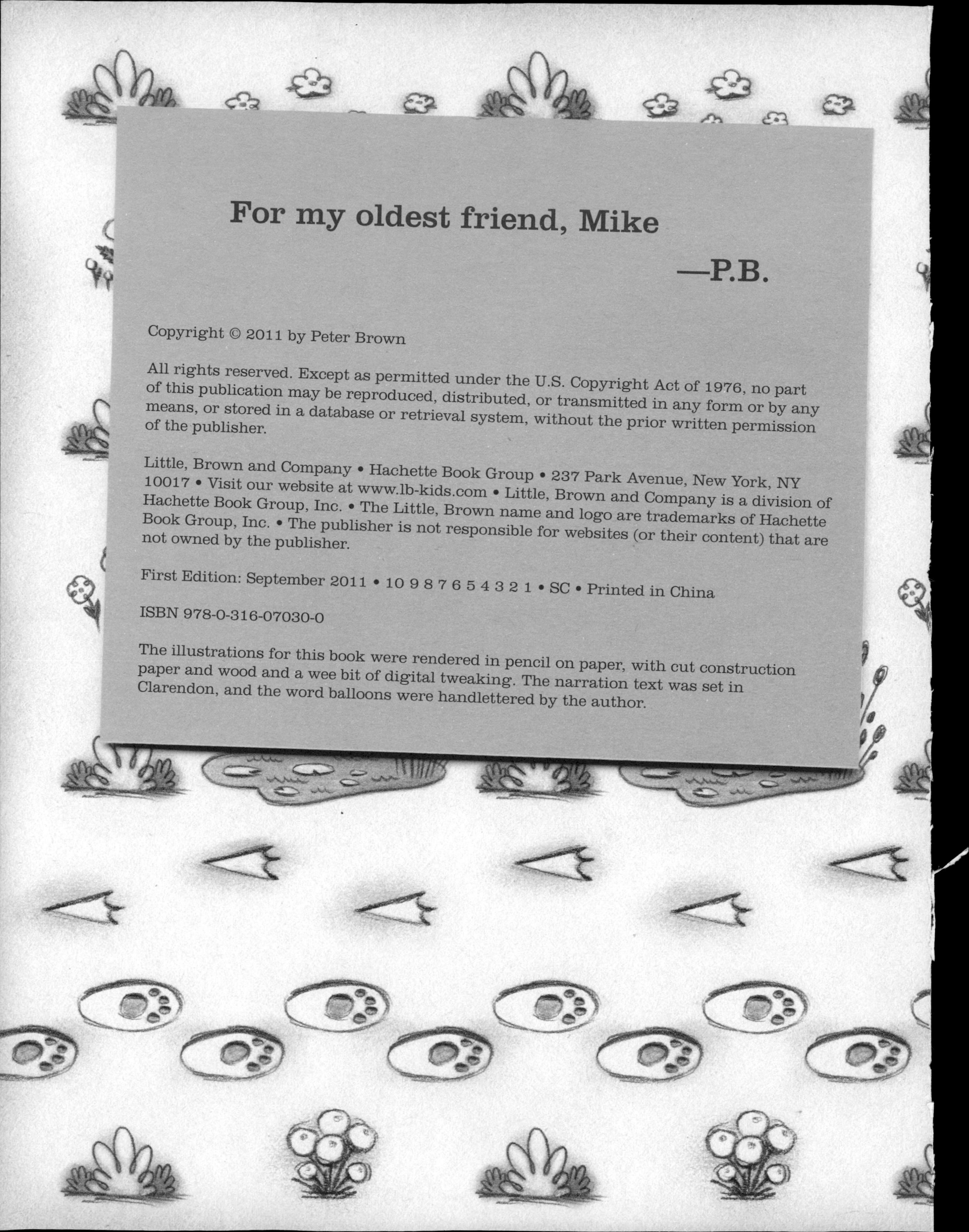

For my oldest friend, Mike

—P.B.

Little, Brown and Company • Hachette Book Group • 237 Park Avenue, New York, NY 10017 • Visit our website at www.lb-kids.com • Little, Brown and Company is a division of Hachette Book Group, Inc. • The Little, Brown name and logo are trademarks of Hachette Book Group, Inc. • The publisher is not responsible for websites (or their content) that are not owned by the publisher.

First Edition: September 2011 • 10 9 8 7 6 5 4 3 2 1 • SC • Printed in China

ISBN 978-0-316-07030-0

The illustrations for this book were rendered in pencil on paper, with cut construction paper and wood and a wee bit of digital tweaking. The narration text was set in Clarendon, and the word balloons were handlettered by the author.